D1087475

DOUBLE, DOUBLE, TWINS AND TROUBLE

WELCOME TO

PECULIAR, PENNSYLVANIA!

A PERFECTLY NICE AND
NOT-AT-ALL CREEPY PLACE TO LIVE

ALSO BY LUNA GRAVES
Thriller Night

WITCHES of PECULIAR

DOUBLE, DOUBLE, TWINS AND TROUBLE

LUNA GRAVES

ALADDIN
NEW YORK LONDON TORONTO SYDNEY NEW DELHI

This book is a work of fiction. Any references to historical events, real people, or real places are used fictitiously. Other names, characters, places, and events are products of the author's imagination, and any resemblance to actual events or places or persons, living or dead, is entirely coincidental.

ALADDIN

An imprint of Simon & Schuster Children's Publishing Division
1230 Avenue of the Americas, New York, New York 10020
First Aladdin hardcover edition July 2022
Text copyright © 2022 by Simon & Schuster, Inc.
Illustrations copyright © 2022 by Laura Catrinella
Also available in an Aladdin paperback edition.
All rights reserved, including the right of reproduction in whole or in part in any form.
ALADDIN and related logo are registered trademarks of Simon & Schuster, Inc.
For information about special discounts for bulk purchases,
please contact Simon & Schuster Special Sales at 1-866-506-1949
or business@simonandschuster.com.
The Simon & Schuster Speakers Bureau can bring authors to
your live event. For more information or to book an event contact
the Simon & Schuster Speakers Bureau at 1-866-248-3049 or visit our
website at www.simonspeakers.com.
Book designed by Heather Palisi
The text of this book was set in Really No. 2.
Manufactured in the United States of America 0622 FFG
2 4 6 8 10 9 7 5 3 1
Library of Congress Cataloging-in-Publication Data
Names: Graves, Luna, author.
Title: Double, double, twins and trouble / by Luna Graves.
Description: First Aladdin paperback edition. | New York : Aladdin, 2022. |
Series: Witches of Peculiar | Summary: In Peculiar, Pennsylvania, the supernatural
kids, from ghosts to werewolves to witches, attend Yvette I. Koffin's Exceptional
School for Supernatural Students (YIKESSS), but while twins Bella and Donna
have great powers, they struggle at controlling their magic.
Identifiers: LCCN 2021032184 (print) | LCCN 2021032185 (ebook) |
ISBN 9781665906234 (hardcover) | ISBN 9781665914260 (paperback) |
ISBN 9781665906241 (ebook)
Subjects: CYAC: Witches—Fiction. | Middle schools—Fiction. | Schools—Fiction. |
Ability—Fiction. | Twins—Fiction. | LCGFT: Paranormal fiction. | Humourous fiction.
Classification: LCC PZ7.1.G7325 Do 2022 (print) | LCC PZ7.1.G7325 (ebook) |
DDC [Fic]—dc23
LC record available at https://lccn.loc.gov/2021032184
LC ebook record available at https://lccn.loc.gov/2021032185

DOUBLE, DOUBLE, DOUBLE, TWINS AND TROUBLE

~~~~~ CHAPTER 1 ~~~~~

Since its founding in 1692 as a safe haven during the witch trials, Yvette I. Koffin's Exceptional School for Supernatural Students has seen its fair share of catastrophe and tomfoolery. Take, for instance, the year 1906, when Gertie the ghoul got stuck inside the faculty gramophone for three days. Or that unfortunate morning in 1844, when a mischievous warlock put sleeping elixir in the potion master's tea to get out of a test and ended up exploding the entire east wing. (Nightshade and caffeine do *not* mix well, it turns out.) It's even rumored that there was a week, in 1717, when the dormitories inexplicably disappeared. Most suspect that particular incident was not a prank but instead had something to do with the veil of protection that hangs over the school grounds, making all magical goings-on invisible to any human that might be passing by.

And yet, despite all the chaos the school has endured over the years, never in the history of YIKESSS has any student caused such widespread destruction as Bella and Donna Maleficent—and on their first day of sixth grade, no less!

It's a dreary Monday in Peculiar, Pennsylvania, when their story begins. An hour ago, before the Maleficent twins set foot in Spell Casting class, the window in Yvette

Koffin's tower framed a view of birds chirping beneath clear, sunny skies. Now, however, a steady rain rattles against the glass, and gusts of wind shriek as they roll through the hemlock trees in the courtyard below.

Unlike the rest of the school, Principal Koffin's office is mostly dry, save for two young witches, soaking wet and sulking on a bench in the center of the room. While the principal is nowhere to be found, a four-eyed crow sits on its perch behind her desk, silent but alert. It has two dark, beady eyes locked on each of the Maleficent twins.

"This is all your fault," Donna says quietly. Her arms are crossed, her gaze fixed straight ahead. A tiny raindrop falls from her chin onto her emerald-green blazer, right in the center of the YIKESSS school crest. It doesn't matter. The blazer, like the rest of her uniform, is already drenched.

"*My* fault?" Bella is wringing the rain out of her long black hair and letting it pool around her feet. There's so much water on the floor already, she figures a little more won't make a difference. "No way, Dee. I was only cleaning up *your* mess."

Dee squeezes her eyes shut. Conjuring those huge, desk-devouring flames in Spell Casting and nearly burning down the school was definitely *not* how her first day as a Real and Powerful Witch was supposed to go. After she'd spent five years trying and failing to blend in at the human school, YIKESSS was supposed to be a fresh start. Her chance to finally be a normal witch.

Bella, on the other hand, has never been satisfied with normal. When the twins came into their powers over the summer and they received their official welcome letter from YIKESSS, Bella assured Dee that sixth grade was going to be *their* year. It didn't matter that nobody liked them at the human school. Now that they had full access to their powers, all the supernatural kids would want to be their friends.

And then Spell Casting happened.

After a lesson on conjuring, Bella and Dee's teacher, Professor Belinda, had the class practicing simple sparks, a spell so easy that even a human could do it. At least that's what Bella said when Dee wasn't getting it right.

"Turn your wrists to a hundred and thirty degrees, Dee," Bella explained, repeating Professor Belinda's words in that annoying, know-it-all tone of hers that made Dee want to zap her own ears off. "No, not like that. Spread your fingers apart, like you're turning a really big doorknob. Here, watch me."

Bella is the older by five minutes and is always telling Dee how things should and should not be done. Or how *she* believes things should and should not be done, anyway.

"But I didn't *need* your help," Dee says now, opening her eyes and slouching farther into the bench. A stray black curl, sopping wet and heavy, falls over her face. She tucks it behind her ear with a huff.

"Oh, you did too," Bella says. "You *always* do."

Dee's jaw drops in outrage. "Do not!"

"Do too!"

Dee fixes Bella with a glare. "I would never even have conjured those flames in the first place if you hadn't distracted me. You're so pushy."

"Pushy?" When the desk they shared caught fire, Bella didn't hesitate. She did what any brave witch would have done in her situation: she *acted*. That wasn't pushy. It was heroic. Besides, she only meant to summon a little rain. It wasn't her fault her magic was so strong that she summoned a storm cloud all the way from Seattle instead.

"A good witch always listens to their instincts," Bella says matter-of-factly. It was one of the first things she learned in *A Beginner's Guide to Witchcraft*, the Level 1 Spell Casting handbook she's already read cover to cover. "And my instincts were telling me I *had* to summon the storm cloud to stop the fire."

"You could've summoned a fire extinguisher," Dee mumbles. "That would have been way less messy."

Bella frowns at Dee, frustrated and a little hurt. Why can't her sister see that she was only trying to help? She looks out the window and starts fiddling with her necklace, a silver crescent moon on a thin chain. It was a first-day-of-school gift from the girls' dads. Dee got one too, except instead of a moon her charm is a gold star. *The moon and stars work together to light up the night,* their dad Antony—or Dad—explained, presenting the twins with two dark jewelry boxes. *Stronger together,* their dad Ron—whom the girls call Pop—added. *Just like the two of you.*

Bella thinks about that crucial moment in Spell Casting, the one when Dee's sloppy wristwork—she looked more like she was swatting a fly than opening a door—made their desk catch fire. Bella remembers staring at the flames, so tall that they grazed the ceiling, and imagining, for one terrifying moment, those flames reaching out like tentacles and snatching Dee away.

So Bella curled her hands into fists, let the fire turn her green eyes red, and thought, *Make it rain*. And rain it did, all over the classrooms, the hallways, and the rest of the school grounds, inside and out. She'd had no idea such a simple spell could be so powerful. By the time Professor Belinda managed to banish the storm outside, the entire first floor of the school was flooded.

On the dark side, at least the fire was out.

"I don't care what you think." Bella flips her wet hair over her shoulder with a flick of her wrist. She's been waiting her whole life to grow into her powers, and now that she has, Dee wants her to feel bad about using them? No way. "I stopped the fire, and I'm not sorry."

Dee rolls her eyes, the same shade of radioactive green as her sister's. Dee knows getting Bella to admit she's wrong is like pulling vampire fangs. Most of the time it's pointless to even try.

Dee sighs and looks down at her black Mary Janes, a brand-new pair for the new school year. When she put them on at breakfast, she imagined all the different places the shoes would take her. To the courtyard, where she could listen to music by the mermaid fountain. To the flyball field for her first broom-flying lesson. To a lunch table in the center of the cafeteria, surrounded by friends. She had not imagined they would bring her here, to the principal's office. She should probably pay extra attention in Clairvoyance class this year.

"When Principal Koffin comes, let me do the talking, okay?" Dee looks at Bella. "We're going to be in enough trouble as it is."

For the first time since they arrived, Bella's brow creases with concern. "You think we'll get in trouble?"

"Duh," Dee says. She looks up at the four-eyed crow, quiet on its perch. Two of its eyes are still watching her, unblinking.

Bella stands up quickly and starts pacing in

small circles. "But it was an accident," she says. Her black boots squeak with every step she takes. The crow uses its other pair of eyes to follow her movements. "We can't be punished for an *accident*."

"We're in the principal's office, Bella," Dee says, shaking her head. "And Principal Koffin is a *harpy*. Haven't you heard what harpy principals do to kids who break the rules?"

Bella stops pacing. "What do they do?"

Dee glances back at the crow, a mischievous look in her eye. Then she sits up straighter and reaches her hands out toward Bella, hooking her fingers like talons. "They snatch them up with their big, birdy claws, fly them back to their nest, and *peck out* their eyes."

Bella's face is skeptical. "Really?"

"No, doofus," Dee says, relaxing into her seat again. "We'll probably just get detention."

Bella's eyes grow wide. "I *can't* get detention," she cries. "It will ruin my chances of getting on Horror Roll!"

Dee shakes her head in disbelief. She's pretty sure Bella loves school more than Dee loves anything. Well, except maybe strawberry milkshakes. And cats. "So you don't get on Horror Roll," Dee says. "Big deal."

"It *is* a big deal!" Bella stomps her foot, and red sparks fly out from beneath her heel. Suddenly the bookcase behind her starts to tremble.

"What's going on?" Dee jumps up. "What did you do?"

"I don't know!" Bella replies, and the trembling intensifies. A stack of books falls from the top shelf and lands with a heavy *thud* just inches from where she stands. Bella lets out a scream of surprise. Around her more furniture starts to shake.

"What does the handbook say about stopping earthquakes?" Dee yells.

"It doesn't!" Bella shouts back. "Natural disasters are Level Two!"

A thick, leather-bound book falls from the middle shelf and grazes Bella's shoulder. She jumps to the side, screams again. That's when Dee realizes: the more Bella panics, the worse the earthquake gets.

"You have to stop freaking out!" Dee says. She extends a hand toward her sister. "Seriously, Bella! *Stop!*"

Blue sparks fly from Dee's fingertips, and a moment later the room goes still and silent. Bella and Dee let out synchronized sighs of relief.

"Wow," Dee says, more to herself than Bella. She pulls her hand back, examines it. Did *she* do that? Fascinated by her fingers, Dee takes a careless step backward and collides with an antique lamp on Principal Koffin's desk. It starts to tip forward.

"Watch out!" Bella calls, pointing over Dee's shoulder.

Dee lunges for the lamp and catches it just before it crashes to the floor, but in her haste she accidentally fires off a giggle charm that hits the four-eyed crow. The bird lets out a string of low, even snickers.

Bella smacks a hand to her forehead. The girls still do not have complete control over their powers and, as such, are no strangers to occasional magical mishaps. "Jeepers creepers, Dee."

Unsure how to reverse the spell, Dee tries the same one that worked on the earthquake. "Stop!" she says, one hand clutching the lamp and the other pointing at the crow. "Stop laughing!"

It doesn't work this time. The bird continues to snicker.

Bella crouches over the fallen books. "Quick, put the lamp back and help me pick these up before—"

The door swings open, and the sisters look up. The rest of Bella's sentence dies in her throat.

Standing ominously in the doorway, her dark red wings filling up the mahogany frame behind her, is Principal Yvette Koffin.

CHAPTER 2

Principal Koffin is tall, even for a harpy. Measuring just over seven feet from the bottom of her taloned toes to the top of her blond head, and with a wingspan nearly double that, she's a perpetually looming presence. She's older than the school, though no one knows exactly how old, and has lived in Peculiar since long before it was even given that name. For centuries she has been walking the halls of YIKESSS with her sharp chin in the air, her hands clasped tightly in front of her, and her dark red wings tucked behind her—resembling a cape. Only those unlucky enough to get on her bad side know how the red goes from dark to bright on the undersides.

Inside her office, wet and frowning, Principal Koffin closes the door behind her. She stretches her wings out wide, casting a shadow over Bella and Dee. A crack of thunder booms outside the window. The four-eyed crow stops its snickering at once.

"Bella and Donna Maleficent." Principal Koffin's voice is stern. "I wish I could say I am surprised to see the two of you here."

The twins exchange a glance. Unfortunately, their reputation as mischief-makers preceded their arrival at YIKESSS. There were a few "incidents" at their human school, magical flare-ups that sometimes occur when a young witch is growing into their powers. Most witches generate little inconveniences—for instance, a disappearing doorknob, or a sneeze that turns their hand blue—but Bella's and Dee's flares were bigger, and much harder to cover up. The humans didn't know exactly how the twins managed to zap their cranky teacher's hair hot pink, or turn the whole school's chalk supply into worms, but everyone suspected that they were involved.

Principal Koffin flaps her wings once, twice, until she's hovering a few feet off the floor. Dee puts the lamp back on the desk and hurries to Bella's side. Bella shrinks back, leaning into her sister for comfort.

"It was an accident, I swear!" Bella covers her face with her hands. "Please, *please* don't give us detention or peck out our eyes!"

Principal Koffin gives Bella a disapproving look. Instead of responding, she flutters her wings quickly, sending tiny droplets of water flying across the room. When she lands on the floor again, she tucks her wings behind her back and smooths down her long red skirt.

Dee puts on a nervous smile. "Um, about the books, and the lamp? We can explain—" she starts, but Principal Koffin interrupts her.

"I saw everything that happened." The principal gives the four-eyed crow a pointed look. "Argus and I have a special connection."

"You mean, like, you can see into his mind?" Bella drops her hands, a look of wonderment on her face.

Principal Koffin, crossing the room to sit behind her desk, nods once. Her movements are so swift and silent that it almost looks like she's floating.

"Creepy!" Bella moves to get a closer look at Argus. "I want one!"

Argus squawks, then flaps his wings and perches on Principal Koffin's shoulder.

"Sit down, girls," Principal Koffin says, and then does so herself. The sisters do as they're told, with Bella perching anxiously on the edge of the bench and Dee slouching into it, more relaxed.

Principal Koffin glances from one twin to the other. "I assume you know why you're here?"

"We do," Bella said. "But like I said before, it was a total *accident*—"

Principal Koffin holds up a hand to silence her. "You do not have to explain it to me. As I said before, I know *everything* that happened. I know about the fire, the storm cloud, and the earthquake."

Dee grimaces. "You do?"

Principal Koffin looks at Argus. She reaches out one long, slender finger and scratches him under the chin. "There are many crows that call YIKESSS home." She looks back at Dee. "And crows love to talk."

"Really?" Bella examines Argus curiously. "Well, what'd they say?"

"They believe that you two did not mean to cause the school any harm. It was, as you said—" Here Principal Koffin raises one sharp eyebrow at Bella. "An accident."

"So does that mean you're not mad?" Bella asks hopefully. Dee looks into two of Argus's eyes and gives him a small smile.

"No," Principal Koffin says. "In fact, I think your display in Spell Casting was quite impressive."

The sisters drop their jaws in unison.

"It has been many years since I have seen such powerful spellwork from witches as young as yourselves," Principal Koffin says. The corner of her mouth turns up into what could *almost* be considered a smile. "Indeed, Bella and Donna Maleficent, I think you will do quite well here."

"Really?" Dee sits up a little straighter. She thinks, again, about that lunch table at the center of the cafeteria. She imagines herself zapping milkshakes from Scary Good Shakes into the hands of all her new friends. She bites her bottom lip to hide her smile.

"So does that mean we won't get detention?" Bella asks.

Principal Koffin nods again. "You will not be receiving any detention today."

Bella breathes out a heavy sigh of relief.

"*But*," Principal Koffin continues, "while your spellwork was impressive, it was also very dangerous. You put your classmates in harm's way, almost destroyed the academy, and risked exposing us to the entire town."

Bella fidgets in her seat. "But it was an—"

"Accidents still have consequences, I'm afraid," Principal Koffin says. "As a result, you two are prohibited from practicing hands-on magic on school grounds for two weeks." As if to emphasize the principal's point, Argus lets out a squawk.

"What?" Bella and Dee say at the same time.

"Two weeks? But that's not fair!" Bella says, jumping out of her seat. Principal Koffin gives her a stern look of warning, and she quickly sits back down. "Can't we have detention instead?"

"Try to understand, girls." Principal Koffin picks up a pair of spectacles and places them

20

on her nose. "Peculiar is a safe haven for the supernatural community, but only because we have gotten so good at hiding in plain sight. What do you think the humans would do if they found out there were monsters living among them?"

Dee shrugs. Despite failing to fit in with her classmates at her last school, she has always had a soft spot for humans. It must be nice not to have to worry that you're going to accidentally destroy the whole town.

"They would cast us out," Principal Koffin continues. A dark look crosses over her face, but she quickly blinks it away.

"But we don't know that for sure," Dee argues. She thinks of one time last year, when a boy in her math class, Peter, watched her sneeze and turn the chalk in her hand into a worm. He was surprised, but as far as she knew, he never told anyone what he saw. That had to count for something. "Things have changed. Humans are more accepting than they used to be."

"Some of them, perhaps, but not all," Principal Koffin says. "So we must be careful."

"We *promise* to be careful," Bella says, her green eyes wide and pleading. "If you just let us do magic, I promise we will *never* risk the safety of the monsters in Peculiar again!"

Principal Koffin fixes her gaze on Bella. Her eyes are magnified behind her spectacles, making them look like dark orbs.

"After the accident today, Professor Belinda had to fly to the news station and bewitch the weatherman so he could explain the storm cloud to the human community. No harm done, really. But what if your next accident is not so easily concealed?"

"But—" Bella whines.

"Do I need to remind you about the council's warning after your last . . . *incident* at your human school?"

"No," Dee says quickly. Bella shakes her head. They're both thinking about the yell-o-gram the Creepy Council sent to their house after the chalk-worm incident. Though Peter never told anyone what happened, the council has spies everywhere. They made it clear that the twins were being watched at school. It wasn't something anyone in the Maleficent family would soon forget.

"*Two* weeks," Principal Koffin says. "And not a word more shall be said on the matter. Take this time to think about the mistakes that were made and consider how they can be avoided in the future."

Bella crosses her arms. "Hmph." She slumps back in her seat like Dee.

Principal Koffin stands up, and Argus returns to his perch. She walks to the small stack of books that fell during the earthquake and gathers them in her arms. Then she flaps her wings and flies to the top of the tall book-case, returning them to their rightful place.

"Patience is a skill, girls," Principal Koffin says from above, her focus no longer on the twins but on organizing the books alphabetically.

"One you would do well to acquaint yourselves with."

The sisters leave Principal Koffin's office feeling defeated. Bella stomps down the spiral staircase back to the main corridor, while Dee trails behind her, quiet except for her growling stomach.

"This is so unfair," Bella grumbles.

"At least it's just two weeks," Dee says. "Hey, when's lunch again?"

"Two weeks is *plenty* of time for us to fall behind," Bella says, snapping her head around. "Don't you want to be the best?"

Dee shrugs. She mainly wants to get through the rest of the day without embarrassing herself. Still, she can't help but replay Principal Koffin's words of encouragement in her mind: *Bella and Donna Maleficent, I think you will do quite well here.*

Bella pushes open the door to the main corridor, and the sisters are met with a wave of clapping and chatter. Bella steps through the doorway and stops in her tracks. Dee, lost in her thoughts of what could be, bumps into Bella's back.

In the middle of the hallway, surrounded by a crowd of students cheering her on, their classmate Crypta Cauldronson is conjuring an arc of perfect blue sparks.

"Oh, for the love of all that's unholy," Bella says with a scowl. "Does she have to show off like that?"

CHAPTER 3

In the cafeteria the Maleficent twins are positively glum. While the incident in Spell Casting has made them the subject of many curious glances and whispered remarks, it hasn't done much to give them any actual friends. As a result, Bella and Dee sit at a table by themselves at the edge of the room, close to one of the big bay windows that face the courtyard gardens. The glass in all the windows at YIKESSS filters out UV rays that would be considered harmful to ghosts, ghouls, and vampires. Outside, the storm still rages on. Dee watches absently as a handful of garden gnomes tend to the flowers, protected from the rain by their little mushroom umbrellas.

"Crypta Cauldronson," Bella says, glaring into her lunch box. "She thinks she's *so* amazing because her mom is president of the Creepy Council." Bella pulls out a banana and slams it down onto the table.

Every monster in Peculiar knows Crypta Cauldronson's mother, Gretchen. Or at least they know her voice. As president of the Creepy Council, she sends out monthly memos detailing the latest community events and supernatural goings-on. There are a variety of ways in which monsters can choose to receive these memos, but in the Maleficent household memos are delivered to the shrunken skull that sits on the living room mantel. Ms. Cauldronson also sends yell-o-grams: warnings delivered right to the ears of monsters who act in ways that threaten to expose the supernatural community to the humans. Rumor has it that the yell-o-grams are usually the secretary's responsibility but Gretchen Cauldronson likes yelling so much that she volunteers to do them herself.

Thanks to Bella's and Dee's flare-ups, the twins have been on the receiving end of three yell-o-grams, each more threatening than the one before. In the yell-o-gram after the chalkworm incident, Ms. Cauldronson warned that if they put the supernatural community at risk one more time, their family would have to leave Peculiar. That means it isn't just Bella's and Dee's futures on the line but their dads' futures as well.

Dee unzips her lunch box, then pulls out a square piece of paper and unfolds it. When she recognizes the handwriting, she grins. "It's a note from Dad and Pop."

Dearest Deedee, we hope you have an amazing first day! Knock 'em dead! But not literally!
We love you,
Dad & Pop
P.S. The green stuff on your sandwich is pesto sauce. It's Ant's new recipe! Try it, you'll like it.

Dee's smile fades. "They're going to be so disappointed." She folds up the note and puts it back inside her lunch box. "They told us to make friends, not natural disasters."

She clutches her star necklace and recalls her dads waving from the doorway that morning as she and Bella walked to the bus stop. Antony is a ghost, so he's translucent, but his smile was so big that she could see it from all the way down the block. And Ron, a werewolf whose human form resembles a huggable lumberjack, was actually wiping away tears. They had never looked so proud.

Bella digs through her lunch box and finds her own note. Instead of reading it, she crumples it up and throws it.

"Really nice," Dee says, frowning at her sister. "Throwing tantrums is a *great* way to make new friends."

The note lands on the floor several feet away, and bounces off the sneaker of a student with light brown skin and dark hair. They're standing in the middle of the aisle, tightly clutching their lunch tray.

"Um." The student looks down at the paper, and then up at Bella and Dee. That's when the twins notice their eyes, the telltale bright red of a vampire. "Did—did you drop this?"

"'Drop' is one way of putting it," Dee says, perking up at the chance to meet someone new. She gets out of her chair and walks over to pick up the paper. "Wow, I love your shoes!"

"Hey," Bella says, studying the vampire as Dee puts the note in front of her again and sits back down. "You okay? You look a little sick."

The vampire shuffles their feet. "My friends on the flyball team are sitting over there," they say, and then look left, toward a table in the center of the room. "And my friends from choir are sitting all the way over there." The vampire looks right, toward the tables by the kitchen. "And I can't decide who I should sit with." They look back at Bella and Dee. "What if I choose wrong and I hurt someone's feelings?"

"Well, you've got to decide sometime," Bella says. She takes the sandwich out of her lunch box and unwraps it. "Or are you going to eat your lunch standing up?" She brings the sandwich closer to her face, studies the bread. "Ew, what's this green stuff?"

"Or you could sit with us?" Dee offers, giving Bella a disapproving look before smiling up at the vampire. "That's what she meant to say."

"Really?" The vampire's bright red eyes dart from Dee to Bella, looking unsure. "You're not saving these for your friends?"

"Jeepers creepers, it's the first day of school,"

Bella says, looking around the room. "How does everybody else have friends already?"

"Probably because they didn't spend their morning in the principal's office," Dee mutters.

The vampire clears their throat. "So, should I . . ."

"Oh!" Bella snaps her head up and scoots her chair over. "Right, sorry. Sit next to me!"

"Okay." The vampire smiles, revealing two pointy white fangs. "Thanks." They put their tray down next to Bella.

"What's your name?" Dee asks, picking up Bella's banana.

"Charlie," they say, and then take a bite of pepperoni pizza. "And by the way, my pronouns are 'they, them.' How about you?"

"Donna," she says. "But call me 'Dee.'"

"And I'm Bella. Our pronouns are 'she, her.'" Bella leans a little closer to Charlie. "We're witches."

"Bella and Donna Maleficent?" A goblin with

light green skin, pointy ears, and orange hair appears, seemingly out of nowhere. His clothes and hair are damp, and he's bouncing in place at the end of their table. "*The* Bella and Donna Maleficent?"

"She prefers 'Dee,'" Charlie says, and Dee smiles into her lap.

"Spooktacular!" the goblin says. "I'm Eugene, and I just wanna say that I think you witches are absolute *legends*. You've gotta tell me all about what went down in Spell Casting."

Dee's smile fades. "You heard about that?"

"Of course! The whole school knows." Eugene sits in the empty seat next to Dee, who sinks farther into her chair with embarrassment. He pulls his green eyephone out of his pocket. The eye opens, and the screen lights up.

"Check this out," he says, and then hands the phone to Dee. It's a video of a classroom caught in the midst of a torrential downpour. Students are scrambling for cover, running into the hallway and ducking under desks.

Above all the screaming, Dee can hear Eugene's commentary from behind the phone. *"Totally crazy! I mean, this rain just came out of nowhere and it's already flooding the room. I wonder if I could turn one of these desks into a rowboat? Oh, snap! Was that thunder? Or was it my stomach? Ha! Man, I'm hungry—"*

Dee puts the eyephone down on the table, groaning. "Great. Who's going to want to be friends with us now?"

"Uh, hello? Me!" Eugene says as Bella snatches up the phone. "Tell me everything. Were the flames really as big as everyone says? Did the desk *just* catch fire, or was there more cool destruction? And what was with all that rain?"

"That was me. *I* summoned a storm cloud all the way from Seattle," Bella chimes in, sliding Eugene's phone back to him. "I'm the one who put the fire out."

Dee shakes her head. Leave it to Bella to brag about their accident now that they aren't in any serious trouble.

"You put it out?" Eugene says, his excitement fading. "Bummer."

"*You're* the one who flooded the school?" Charlie says, shocked at Bella. "My socks are soaked because of you!"

Bella crosses her arms, scowling at them both, and Dee feels a wicked sort of satisfaction.

"Hey, you're witches," Eugene says. "Can you zap us dry?"

Bella snorts. "Don't you think that if we could zap ourselves dry, we would've done it by now?"

Dee meets Bella's eyes and frowns. Dee mouths, *Be nice.* In response Bella sticks out her tongue.

"What Bella means to say," Dee chimes in, "is that we aren't allowed. We got banned from doing magic on school grounds for two weeks." Not to mention, she doubts whether they even have enough control over their powers to successfully pull off a spell like that. But she decides to keep that part to herself.

"That's totally unfair!" Eugene says.

"I don't know," Charlie says nervously. "Maybe it's for the best. I mean, no offense, but I don't think I can handle any more surprises. My stomach is *way* too sensitive for that."

"BOO!"

A translucent ghost in a suit and top hat pops up in the middle of the table, making Charlie and Dee scream and jump in their seats. The ghost, whom the students now recognize as their vice principal, Augustus "Gus" Archaic, keels over in a fit of laughter.

"Oh!" he says between giggles. "Oh! I got you!"

"A ghost who says 'boo'?" Bella asks, looking unimpressed. "Kind of unoriginal, don't you think?"

Vice Principal Archaic twiddles his handlebar mustache. "Perhaps. But still a highly effective form of scaring." He points at Charlie, who looks a little green. "I mean, just look how scared they are!"

Dee gives Charlie a sympathetic look. She is not a fan of being scared either. If Vice Principal Archaic were a spider, or a creepy doll, Dee would be halfway across the cafeteria by now.

"Vice Principal Archaic," Bella says. She points at a table near the center of the cafeteria, where Crypta Cauldronson is seated. "I think that table could use a good scare, don't you?"

"Excellent idea, Miss Maleficent." Vice Principal Archaic rubs his hands together. "Oh, I do love keeping you students on your gnarly toes!"

He disappears. A moment later Crypta's scream cuts through the cafeteria chatter. Bella grins, then takes a big bite of her sandwich.

"Does he always do that?" Dee asks, looking warily after the vice principal.

"Unfortunately," Charlie says. They push their tray into the center of the table, their appetite gone. "This morning I saw him jump out of a water fountain in the crypts. He scared Trixie Fae half to death." They glance from Dee to Bella. "There was pixie dust *everywhere*."

"I heard he's been scaring since the beginning of time," Eugene adds. "You know that one painting of the screaming man?" He puts his hands on his cheeks and drops his jaw, mimicking someone about to let out a bloodcurdling scream. "Apparently, Archaic is the one who scared the man."

"Well, he's not going to scare me," Bella says, still munching on her sandwich. As it turns out, she quite likes the green stuff on the bread. "I'm unscareable. I'm going to be the next Bloody Mary."

"No way," Eugene says. Every monster knows the legend of Bloody Mary, but few have been lucky enough to meet her in person. She's quite elusive and can only be summoned by great power or extreme fear. "Have you ever met her?"

"Not yet," Bella admits. She thinks about all the hours she has spent in front of the bathroom mirror with the lights off, holding a candle and chanting Mary's name. It has never worked. "But I will one day."

"Don't beat yourself up." Eugene shrugs. "Wanting to be the next Bloody Mary, though? That's, like, the toughest gig to get."

Bella glares at him. "You don't think I'm scary enough?" She puts her long black hair in front of her face and tilts her head down, giving Eugene a menacing look. "How about now?"

"You're terrifying!" Charlie says, and then puts their head in their hands.

"So, Eugene," Dee says, changing the subject before Charlie passes out. "You're really into fire, huh?"

"Not just fire," he says, smirking. "I'm into mischief of *all* kinds."

"Like what?" Bella asks, fixing her hair.

"Like experiments, and explosions." Eugene gives them a proud smile. "Last month I built a waterslide in my bedroom." His smile dims a little. "That one didn't work out the way I'd hoped."

"An indoor waterslide?" Bella is skeptical. "You made that all by yourself?"

"Oh, yeah," he says. "Hey, you ghouls wanna come to my house after school and see what I'm working on now?" He leans in eagerly, lowers his voice. "Think 'jetpack,' but with whoopie cushions."

"Creepy," Dee says, smiling wide. She and Bella have never been invited to a friend's house before. That boy Peter, from the human school, once invited their entire class to the community pool for a birthday party, but Bella and Dee's dads said they couldn't go. Apparently, budding witches were supposed to avoid chlorine. Then someone started a rumor that the twins were afraid of the water, and nobody invited them to any more pool parties. Or parties of any kind.

"Yeah," Bella agrees. "It sounds like something I'll have to see for myself."

"Me too," Charlie adds. "As long as nothing is going to jump out at me."

"Wicked!" Eugene springs up. "This is gonna be awesome!"

Bella and Dee look at each other, exchanging a small smile. Each sister knows what the other is thinking. Their morning might have gotten off to a rough start, but now look at them, making new friends! Just like they promised their dads they would.

The sisters finish their lunches, feeling hopeful again. Maybe their first day as Real and Powerful Witches isn't completely ruined, after all.

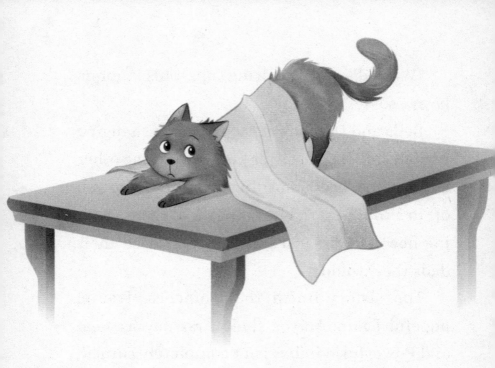

CHAPTER 4

While some YIKESSS students, like Charlie, live on campus, others, such as the twins and Eugene, commute from home. And where is *home* if you're a monster in the suburbs, trying to hide in plain sight?

Welcome to Eerie Estates.

For generations most of the supernatural community in Peculiar has lived in a gated housing development called Eerie Estates. The matching two-story homes, painted in the most cheerful shades of boysenberry and black, were built in the 1800s in the Gothic style, and then renovated with modern appliances in the 1960s. The original architect was a centaur who greatly valued his privacy, so his final, most important touch was to enclose the estates in layers of tall, dense shrubbery. Not even the nosiest joggers or dog walkers passing by have been able to glimpse what goes on inside.

Of course, most might think: *Eerie Estates— could they* be *any more obvious?* But supernatural creatures are not, nor have they ever been, known for their subtlety. Why else would there be so many legends and myths about them? And too many of them wholly unflattering! Why do humans never talk about the venerable and lifesaving zombie doctor who studied for his degree by practicing on himself?

But truly, when it comes to Eerie Estates, there's no need to worry. Most humans in Peculiar assume that the name of the estates is simply a misspelling of "Erie," a nearby town, and residents don't bother correcting them.

Now, back to the young witches.

After school Bella, Dee, and Charlie follow Eugene back to his house in Eerie Estates. The Seattle storm has passed, but gray skies still hang overhead.

"I'm gonna call Dad and Pop and tell them where we're going," Dee says to Bella. She pulls her blueteeth out of their pouch in her backpack and sticks them into her mouth. The device, which resembles a retainer from human dentistry and features the latest supernatural technology, allows Dee to communicate with her dads through her thoughts. It also makes her look like she has blue teeth.

She thinks about calling her dad Ron. A

moment later she hears his voice inside her mind.

Deedee?

Hi, Pop!

Is everything okay?

Everything is great! I just wanted to tell you that Bella and I are going to a friend's house for a little while.

A friend? That's wonderful, hon! Who's the lucky monster?

They arrive at Eugene's house. A sign that reads STUFF & FLUFF TAXIDERMY in fancy cursive is staked into the grass in the front yard.

His name is Eugene, Dee thinks. *His house is just a couple of streets over from ours. And we made another friend, Charlie. They're here too.*

Dee glances over at Charlie, who's keeping a comfortable distance from the wooden stake.

Oh, Dee. Dad and I are so happy you and Bells are making friends.

Me too. Tell you about it later, okay?

Absolutely. Love you.

Love you, too.

"Taxidermy?" Bella studies the sign, eyes widening. "As in, stuffing dead animals?"

"You got it," Eugene says, leading them up the driveway. "The family business." His smile dims a little when he says it.

Dee puts the blueteeth away and looks at Eugene. "You don't want to be a taxidermist?"

Eugene shakes his head. "It's more my parents' thing. They're zombies, so it's kind of a perfect job for them. You know, because they like to pickle the brains and save them for later."

"Gross," Charlie moans. "I think I'm going to be sick."

"Hey, no need to be rude." Eugene glances back at them as he opens the front door. "I don't judge your bloodsucking habits, do I?"

"Oh, of course," Charlie says, throwing up their hands. "You assume that just because I'm a vampire, I like to drink blood?"

"Well," Bella says, raising an eyebrow. "Don't you?"

"No!" Charlie crosses their arms. "It's disgusting! *Way* too sweet."

"Don't worry, Mom and Dad aren't home. And even if they were, they keep all the organs and stuff locked up in the back." Eugene steps inside and gestures for them to follow. "Come on, I'll give you ghouls a tour."

They all put their backpacks down by the door and look around the room. Lots of beige, Bella notices with a frown, and very sparsely furnished. There's not a single cauldron or crystal ball in sight.

Eugene guides them from the living room through the dining room, and then through a doorway into the kitchen. Aside from the jar of pickled fingers on the counter, these rooms also look like ones in a regular human house. Neither of the twins can even pretend to be impressed.

"It has to look boring so our human customers don't get suspicious when they pick up their pets," Eugene explains after a long period of silence.

Dee's eyes widen. "You mean your parents let humans come into your house?" She would have loved to invite Peter and some of the other human kids from her class over to her house, but her dads never would have allowed it. It was, as they always said, too big a risk.

"Sometimes." Eugene shrugs. "They're not so bad, you know. Aside from their weird taste in furniture."

Eugene leads his guests up the stairs and into his bedroom. It's much more colorful than the other rooms in the house and is littered everywhere with a bunch of random trinkets and half-completed experiments.

"And this is where the magic happens," Eugene says. Bella, Dee, and Charlie all frown.

"I didn't know goblins could do magic," Bella says, still bitter about her suspension.

"Not real magic," Eugene says. "These are all my inventions." He gestures to the floor, which is covered with a plastic tarp. "This is where I built the waterslide. Um, my parents are still fixing the floors." He moves to his desk, where a towel is draped over something basketball-sized. "And this"—he pulls off the towel to reveal a decked-out backpack—"is the Toot-master 6000. Observe."

Eugene puts on the backpack and presses a red button attached to a strap. The backpack lets out a loud, whoopie-cushion-style fart noise and then shoots him into the air, making him bonk his head on the ceiling.

"Still working out the kinks," Eugene says, laughing nervously. A second later the engine sputters out and he falls to the floor. Lying faceup on the tarp, he raises a thumb. "I'm okay!"

Dee helps Eugene stand up. "Failure is just part of success," she says encouragingly. "Thomas Edison failed a thousand times before he got the lightbulb to work."

Eugene looks confused. "Is that a human?"

Charlie picks up the backpack. "You know," they say, examining it, "if you get this thing to work, you could join the flyball team." They pause, considering. "Though you'll probably have to take out the whoopie cushions."

"Absolutely not!" Eugene says, grabbing the Tootmaster out of Charlie's arms and hugging it in his own. "The whoopie cushions are the most important part!"

Bella puts her hands on her hips. "As a future member of the scream team, who will be cheering at *all* the flyball games, I *forbid* you to use that thing on the field."

"A future member?" Charlie asks.

"Tryouts are tomorrow," Bella explains, beaming. "But I know I'll make it. I've been practicing my screams all summer."

"She has." Dee meets Charlie's gaze and frowns. "Every. Single. Day. And did I mention we share a room?"

"That's brutal," Eugene says, and Bella glowers. "So should we move on with the tour? I can't *wait* to show you the bathroom."

Bella and Dee scrunch up their noses in unison.

"I want to see the taxidermy animals," Bella says. "I bet there's lots of creepy dead stuff in there."

"You know, I totally would show you," Eugene says, running a hand through his poufy orange hair. "But I'm not supposed to take anybody into the lab. My parents put a lock on the door, and they have the key."

"Well, that settles it," Charlie says. "No dead animals for us. *Rats*."

"Dee and I could zap the lock open," Bella suggests, twirling a strand of her hair around her finger. "It would be a simple untethering spell." Next to her, Charlie frowns.

"No way," Dee says. "Or did you already forget what happened in Spell Casting, the last time we tried to do a 'simple' spell?" She puts air quotes around "simple."

Eugene shakes his head. "The lock is magic-proof anyway. The only way we're getting in there is if someone picks it the old-fashioned way."

"We can't do that!" Charlie says. "We're monsters, not criminals!"

Bella looks meaningfully at Eugene. "Aren't goblins really good at picking locks?"

"Well, yeah," Eugene says, looking bashfully at the floor. "I *could* do it, but—"

Bella interrupts him, her eyes bright with an idea. "But I thought you said you liked mischief of *all* kinds?"

Eugene looks up. He gives Bella a wicked smirk. "You're on." He leads Bella, Dee, and Charlie down the stairs to the first floor, and to the back of the house. They stop in front of the basement door, which is bolted shut with a large iron lock.

"This will only take a minute," Eugene says. He kneels down and starts fiddling with the lock.

"One minute?" Bella says, unconvinced. "Fat chance. I'll time you. One, two, three—"

"Done!" The lock falls off, and Eugene stands up.

"Whoa," Dee says. "Impressive."

"It wasn't *that* impressive," Bella mutters.

The group follows Eugene down the basement steps and into the lab. Eugene flips the light switch, and Dee screams.

"What are all those creepy dolls doing down here?" she cries, hiding behind Bella. Indeed, filling the shelves on the back wall are dozens of dolls, all varying in shape, size, and anatomy. Dee is particularly disturbed by one with a few extra legs sewn into the sides, which looks to her like a doll-spider hybrid. She squeezes her eyes shut.

"Mom and Dad use them to practice their stitching," Eugene says, moving toward the operating table in the middle of the room. "They practice every day. It's why they're the best taxidermists in town."

Bella looks around the room, taking in the dolls, the overflowing filing cabinets, and the taxidermy specimens that line the walls. She sees animals of all kinds, domestic and wild.

There are even a couple of dodo birds, and one small yellow dragon next to the room's only window, which lets in just a small sliver of light. Even though the window is open, the lab still feels to her a little like a crypt. It's the perfect work space for a zombie.

"I was right," Bella says. She wanders around the room and touches each stuffed animal she passes. "There is a *lot* of creepy dead stuff down here."

"Oh, yeah," Eugene brags. "Business is *booming*. And believe it or not, most of our customers are humans. They all come get their poodles preserved after the dogs die." He makes a face like, *Can you believe it?*

"Yuck," Dee says. She notices three stuffed poodles to her left and shudders. She can't imagine doing that to something she loves.

Charlie hovers by the bottom of the stairs. "If I'm being honest, dead things freak me out. I don't like to confront my own immortality."

Bella notices a big lump under a white sheet

sitting atop the operating table. She takes a step closer, reaches out her hand. "Is this what your parents are working on now?"

"Don't touch it!" Eugene jumps in between Bella and the lump. "It's bad enough we're down here at all. Mom and Dad will kill me if I mess anything up."

"I *won't* mess anything up," Bella assures him.

"Famous last words," Dee says. She sits on the bottom step next to Charlie. "I'm with Eugene. You shouldn't touch it."

Bella purses her lips. "I just want to get a closer look," she says, more to herself than anyone else. "That's all." She steps around Eugene and lifts up the sheet, revealing a plump orange fur ball. A dead cat wearing a collar that reads CORNELIUS.

"There," Eugene says. "You've had a closer look."

"Hmm." She taps her chin. "He's actually pretty cute. But his fur is looking a little dull."

"I'll let Mom know," Eugene says. "Now if you could just cover him back up—"

Instead of covering him up, Bella leans in closer. She puts one hand over the cat and touches his fur with the tips of her fingers. She frowns. "Not very soft, either."

"Bella!" Dee warns. "Knock it off!"

"Oh, come on." Bella straightens up. "It's dead. What could I possibly do?"

"Oh, I dunno," Eugene says. "For one thing, you could use your witchy powers to bring it back to *life*?" He pauses, laughs uncomfortably. "Uh, please don't do that."

Bella snorts. "Necromancy is Level Five, Eugene. Everybody knows that."

She picks up the white sheet. As she drapes it over the cat, she imagines regretfully how much better it would look with brighter and softer fur, the way it probably looked when it was still alive. She feels a tickle of fur graze her thumb, and before she even realizes what's happening, white sparks shoot out from her fingertips and into the cat. Its body jolts, like it's been electrified, and then goes still.

The whole room is stunned. Bella yanks her hand back and grimaces at Eugene. "It was an accident?"

"Maleficent!" His eyes dart from the cat to Bella and back again. "What did you do?"

Bella shrugs. "I'm not really sure." They all pause a moment to look at the cat. It's quiet under the sheet.

"Great work, Bella," Dee says, her head in her hands. "You killed the cat a second time."

Then the cat sits up, poking its head out from under the sheet. It blinks slowly and looks around. It lets out one long, moaning meow.

Bella winces. "Oops."

"It's alive!" Dee jumps up. "You zapped it back to life!"

"You zapped it back to life," Eugene repeats, grabbing the sides of his hair. "After I specifically asked you not to!"

"I didn't do it on purpose!" Bella says. "I

wasn't even *trying* to cast a spell. It just happened." At this she feels a small wave of excitement, even though she *is* sorry. There's power inside her she has yet to explore.

"Okay, it's okay. Everyone try to stay calm," Charlie says. They're pacing in small circles and taking quick, panicked breaths. "Stay! Calm! ACHOO!" They stop pacing, rub their nose. "Sorry. Cat allergy."

The cat meows again. It stands up and does a long stretch across the table.

"This is *not* a big deal," Bella says. She walks to the bookcase next to the creepy dolls and pulls a thick leather book off the shelf. "I can just knock it right back out."

"You will not!" Dee runs over to her sister and yanks the book from her hand. She's a softie when it comes to all creatures, but especially cats.

Bella makes a face. "You know I can just get another book off the shelf."

"ACHOO." Charlie sneezes again.

"No, Dee is right," Eugene says. "This cat died from old age. If we knock it out, my parents will know we messed with the taxidermy specimen, and I'll be grounded for the rest of my life."

"Well, what's your idea?" Bella snaps. "We can't just leave it alive."

"We can't kill it!" Dee cries. "It's an innocent little kitty!"

"Little?" Eugene says. "Dee, just curious. What do you think the word 'little' means?"

"Um, guys," Charlie shouts. They point at the back wall, toward the basement's one window. "I hate to interrupt, but the cat is escaping!"

The kids all turn their heads just in time to see the cat jump from the top of the filing cabinet to the small window. As it struggles to squeeze its backside through, Dee tries to zap it into her arms with a spell, but it escapes. The spell bounces off the glass and hits the creepy spider doll instead.

"Ah!" Dee screams, realizing that the spider

doll is now in her arms. She drops it, and it lands on the concrete with a thud that makes the room go silent.

Everyone turns to glare at Bella.

"Well," Bella says sheepishly. "Now what?"

CHAPTER 5

"Oh no," Eugene says, still pulling his hair. His usually pointy ears have gone droopy. "Oh no, oh no, oh no!"

"Jeepers creepers, Eugene," Bella says, leaning against the shelves with the dolls. "You've got to calm down." She looks at Charlie, who is still unsuccessfully taking deep, calming breaths. "You too."

"Calm down?" Eugene yells. "CALM DOWN?"

Bella nods.

"My parents are going to kill me!" Eugene says. "I'm not supposed to bring friends down here, *ever*, because of situations exactly like this one!"

Despite everything going on, hearing Eugene call them his friends lifts Dee's spirits a little. She was worried that Bella had ruined their chances. Now, no matter what happens next, at least she knows they still have one another.

"They're going to be home soon," Eugene continues. "And then they're going to *kill* me. And then, because they're zombies, I'll come back to life. And then they'll kill me again!"

"We can still fix this," Dee says, placing a hand on his shoulder. "We just have to find the cat. It couldn't have gone far, right?"

"It's probably going home for dinner," Bella says. "It hasn't eaten since it died. I'll bet it's starving."

Dee frowns. It's a long shot, but it's all they have. "How are we supposed to know where it lives?"

"My parents keep a record of every customer," Eugene says. He's pulled at his hair so much that it's sticking straight out on the sides. He looks like a mad scientist. "In that filing cabinet, over there."

Bella and Dee both run to the filing cabinet and start rifling through the drawers.

"So." Charlie, still pacing in small circles, is now sweating profusely. They take off their uniform jacket and tie it around their waist. "Once we figure out who the owner is, all we have to do is find the cat and catch it before the owner realizes their dead cat isn't so dead anymore."

"Exactly," Dee says.

Charlie groans. They bend over and put their hands on their knees. "I feel woozy."

"Want some water?" Eugene asks. "Or some plasma?"

"Got it!" Bella pulls out a file labeled CORNELIUS. She opens the file and starts shuffling through the papers inside. A Polaroid photo falls out of the stack onto the floor. "This paperwork was turned in two days ago by . . ." Her eyes skim over the words on the page.

Dee picks up the Polaroid. It's a picture of the orange cat—Cornelius—curled up next to a boy with dark brown skin and a big smile. The date written on the back of the photo is from two years ago.

"Cute." Dee smiles. She tucks the Polaroid into her pocket.

"Uh-oh," Bella says. She looks around at the group. "We've got a problem."

Charlie stands upright. "You mean *besides* the problems we already have?"

Bella nods.

"The cat belongs to a human, doesn't it?" Eugene starts pulling at his hair again. "I should've guessed."

"Not just any human." Bella looks at Dee.

Dee glances at the paperwork over her sister's shoulder, and then lets out a gasp.

"Cornelius belongs to Boris Smith? No!" Dee says.

"The human mayor of Peculiar?" Eugene drops his hands and goes still. "Holy hobgoblins. I am so dead."

"The mayor!" Charlie cries. "If he finds out what we've done, all the monsters in Peculiar will be in danger!" Their red eyes roll to the back of their head and they fall to the floor, unconscious.

Bella, Dee, and Eugene all exchange a panicked look.

"We need to find Cornelius," Dee says. "And fast."

Bella rips a corner off a piece of paper and holds it up. "I've got the mayor's address," she says, then puts the paper into the pocket of her blazer. "It's on the other side of town." Eugene watches her do it with a defeated look on his face.

"Fine," he says. "Let's go."

"Wait." Dee hurries over to Charlie, who's slowly sitting up on the floor. "First we should make sure Charlie is okay. Eugene, will you get them some water?"

"Actually"—Charlie glances from Eugene to the stuffed dragon and back again—"do you think your parents have any dragon plasma?"

Bella furrows her brow. "Seriously?"

"What?" Charlie says. "It's got *tons* of electrolytes."

CHAPTER 6

C ornelius!"

"Here, kitty, kitty!"

The Maleficent twins wander down Franken Lane with their backpacks on and their hands cupped over their mouths, calling out for the lost cat. A few paces behind them, Eugene texts his mom to tell her he's going into town with friends, while Charlie sips from their thermos of dragon plasma.

"I'm feeling better already," Charlie says, holding up the thermos to Eugene. "Tell your parents thanks for me."

"I'll be sure to do that," Eugene says, putting his eyephone into his pocket. "Right after they kill me for sneaking into the lab, reviving the cat, and then *losing* the cat."

"We haven't lost it," Bella says, her tone forcefully optimistic. "We've temporarily mis-placed it."

"Stop calling the cat an 'it,'" Dee says. "He has a name." She cups her hands back over her mouth and shouts again. "Cornelius!"

"Who's askin'?"

A big green ogre washing his car two drive-ways down turns in their direction, a confused look on his face. "Whadda you kids want?"

"Sorry, Mr. Grunk," Eugene says, waving in apology. "We're looking for a cat. He has the same name as you."

"Hmph." The ogre returns to hosing down his Prius.

"That guy's name is Cornelius?" Dee raises an eyebrow.

"Yeah," Eugene says. "And he'll put anything in his 'everything stew,' even if it's undead. So we'd better hurry."

"What exactly is our plan?" Charlie says between sips of plasma. "Even if we can find the cat, how will we catch him?"

"Magic," Bella says. "Duh."

Eugene sighs. "Anybody else have a better plan? Something more . . . reliable?"

Bella gives him an irritated glance. "My magic is reliable."

"Reliably *unreliable*," Dee says, which makes Eugene and Charlie laugh.

Instead of replying, Bella curls her hands into fists, clenches her teeth, and focuses very hard on the road ahead, trying to stay calm. Suddenly the stop sign at the end of the block bursts into flames.

"Oh!" Bella shouts. She relaxes her fists, and the fire disappears. She glances back at the rest of the group. They're all silent, mouths agape.

"Um." Bella laughs nervously. "I totally meant to do that."

They arrive at the intersection of Franken Lane and Stein Street and make a left, toward the front gate of Eerie Estates. In the distance a werewolf lets out a long, moaning howl. The twins wonder absently if it's their dad Ron, who has been known to howl after a particularly long day of work at the pharmacy.

"I know! Cats love catnip," Dee says, thinking about their neighbor's cat, Moonpie, and her favorite catnip treats shaped like little fish. "We should go to the pet store and get some. Then we won't have to catch Cornelius. We'll shake the container, and he'll come to us."

"I like that idea," Charlie says. They tip the thermos upside down and empty the last of the dragon plasma into their mouth. "It's very logical."

"How do we know Cornelius even likes catnip?" Bella interjects. "He's not a regular cat—he's undead."

"So?" Dee says.

"*So* maybe he doesn't like regular cat stuff," Bella says. "I think we should go to the market and get some meat or fish. Maybe some smoked turkey, or canned tuna. Whichever is smellier."

"Here we go again." Dee rolls her eyes.

Bella frowns. "What is that supposed to mean?"

Behind the sisters, Eugene and Charlie exchange a nervous glance.

"We always have to do what you want to do," Dee says. "You never listen to my ideas."

Bella is quiet as she tries to recall the last time she went along with one of Dee's ideas. When she can't think of a time, she simply says, "That's not true."

"Yes, it is," Dee argues. "I said it wasn't a good idea to mess with the cat, but you did it anyway. And look what happened!" They pass an old woman in a pointy witch hat, rocking back and forth in a chair on her front porch. Dee momentarily drops her anger and waves brightly at her. "Hi, Mrs. Cromwell!"

"I didn't cast the spell on purpose," Bella says, ignoring Mrs. Cromwell. "It just happened! Jeepers creepers, how many times do I have to say it? You're the one who never listens to me! Not in the basement, not now, and definitely not in Spell Casting—"

"Of *course* I listened to you in Spell Casting," Dee interrupts. "I couldn't help but listen to you. You wouldn't stop talking! That's why I messed up the spell in the first place."

"Oh really?" Bella bites back. "Do you really want to go there?"

"I don't," Eugene says.

"Me either," Charlie agrees.

"You messed up the spell because you had sloppy form!" Bella says. "Being a good witch requires practice, precision, and patience!" She lists them off on her fingers. "The three *P*s!"

"Oh, stop quoting the handbook!" Dee says with an exaggerated eye roll.

"Hey, witches," Eugene says cautiously. "What if—"

"I didn't need you to butt in during Spell Casting," Dee says to Bella, cutting off Eugene. "And I don't need you to butt in now. I know more about cats than you do, and I think we should get the catnip."

"Well, I know more about magical creatures than you do," Bella says. "And I think we should get meat or fish."

"Hey!" Eugene yells. Everyone turns to look at him. "I have an idea. How about we split up? Dee and Charlie can go to the pet store for some catnip, and I'll go with Bella to the market. Then we can meet at the mayor's place, and we'll be extra prepared."

Bella purses her lips, considering. "Fine.

And then, when it turns out I'm right, Dee has to apologize."

Dee narrows her eyes. "You mean when *I'm* right, you have to apologize to me."

Up in the sky, the sun peeks out from behind a cloud.

"Shoot," Charlie says, feeling the heat on their skin. They reach into the pocket of their blazer and pull out a small black tube. They look down at the thermos in their hand, then up at Eugene. "Can you hold this for a minute?"

Eugene takes the thermos. Charlie unscrews the tube's cap and squeezes white goo into the palm of their hand.

"What is that stuff?" Eugene asks, watching Charlie rub the goo on their face. "Sunscreen?"

"Sunscream. It's for vampires." Charlie holds up the tube, revealing the Sunscream logo in red letters.

"Our dads have that at the apothecary," Bella says. "It's a big seller."

"Your parents run the apothecary?" Eugene asks. "That's pretty sick."

"It's also called a pharmacy," Dee adds proudly. "If you happen to ask a human."

Dee likes to assist her dads at the store—unpacking shipments, shelving items, helping customers find whatever oddities they're looking for. Especially the humans. Just last week she learned about cherry-flavored cough drops. *Fascinating* stuff.

"That's where I got this Sunscream from," Charlie says, rubbing the goo onto the tips of their ears. "Your dads' shop is the only place in town that carries it."

Dee's smile falters. She thinks about the council's yell-o-gram warning: one more slipup, and they'll have to leave Peculiar forever. That means their dads would have to give up the pharmacy, and then Charlie wouldn't have anywhere to buy their Sunscream.

They have to find Cornelius—*fast*.

The group arrives at the front gate. Tall

and spiked, the gate resembles a solid iron door and is a looming barrier between Eerie Estates and the humans who live beyond it. It's impossible to climb, though a few have tried, and is enchanted to open for any supernatural creature who wants to pass through. Any humans must be given prior approval and be accompanied by a supernatural chaperone at all times.

Bella places her palm on the gate. It opens immediately.

"Should we take the bus?" She looks at the empty bus stop by the graveyard across the street. It's no coincidence that Eerie Estates is located across from the oldest, spookiest graveyard in Peculiar. Graveyards are to monsters what playgrounds are to humans: places to haunt, howl, and hang out without raising too much suspicion. And the older the graveyard the better. When humans stop coming to grieve, the dead (and undead) have more space to move around.

"The pet store is right around the corner," Dee says, relieved at the chance to get a break from her sister. "Charlie and I can walk."

Charlie, who has moved on to applying Sunscream to their hands, nods in agreement.

"The market is closer to the mayor's house." Eugene looks at Bella. "We should take the bus to get there faster."

"Fine," Bella says. She kicks a rock across the street.

"Fine," Dee repeats, and then crosses her arms.

The young monsters step through the gate, and it closes behind them.

~~~~·•❀ CHAPTER 7 ❀•·~~~~

The pet store is mostly free of humans when Dee and Charlie arrive. Charlie goes off in search of catnip, but Dee thinks Cornelius might also be tempted by some toys. She wanders to the back of the store in search of some fuzzy mice, but instead gets distracted by the live animals. When Charlie finds her again, Dee is crouching down, watching two cuddly gerbils nap together in their cage.

"Dee?" Charlie jiggles the catnip shaker in front of her face. "Earth to Dee? I found the catnip. Did you get the toys?"

Dee blinks. "Sorry. I got distracted." She points at the snoozing gerbils. "Look how cute they are!"

Charlie wrinkles their nose. "I don't really like rodents."

Dee stands up. "I thought bats were rodents."

"Excuse me." Charlie crosses their arms. "I am not a *regular bat*. I'm a vampire bat. And I'm still getting the hang of it."

"Sorry," Dee says. "If it makes you feel any better, I'm not exactly an expert-level witch yet either." She and Bella made more mistakes in one day than most witches did in their entire lives. Not to mention she was already behind on her classes given they spent so much time in Principal Koffin's office today.

"You'll get there," Charlie says. "You can

conjure flames and stop earthquakes. And it's still only your first day of training." They give her a pat on the back. "Come on, cat toys are in aisle two."

Dee and Charlie walk to aisle two, where they discover a large wall of cat toys in a variety of shapes and sizes. Dee picks out a few fuzzy mice, plus a wand with a red ribbon. She eyes a Swiss-cheese plushy. "Do you think Cornelius would like one of these?"

"I think all the toys you've got in your hands should be plenty," Charlie says. They lean in to get a better look at the block of cheese. "Wait, can you put catnip in there?"

Dee grabs the block of cheese and adds it to the top of her pile. "I can't believe Bella doesn't think this will work," she scoffs. "She just likes her plan best because she's the one who came up with it. She's such a know-it-all."

"I think your plan is great," Charlie says. "Don't worry about what Bella thinks."

"Thank you," Dee says. "I just don't get why she always has to be the boss of everything."

Charlie sighs, then wanders down the aisle, past the dog toys and the treats. Dee follows along, still talking.

"She's been like this since we were little. She thinks that because she's five minutes older, she's always right."

Charlie nods, saying nothing.

"It's so annoying," Dee continues. "Do you know what it's like to grow up with a sister who always pushes you around? Who criticizes everything you do? Who borrows your *underwear*?"

Dee frowns. There's a lot she can tolerate from Bella, but the underwear thing is just so *ew*.

Charlie and Dee linger at the end of the aisle, by the collars and leashes. Dee picks up a green kitty collar with a little bell attached, thinking about how cute Cornelius would look in it.

Then she puts it back down. *Don't get attached,* she reminds herself. She glances at Charlie, who has gone quiet.

"Everything okay?" She nudges them with her elbow.

"Yeah," Charlie says. "I was just thinking . . . I don't know what it's like to have a sister."

"You mean you don't have any siblings?" Dee asks, thinking that being an only child sounds kind of nice right now.

Charlie shakes their head. "It's just me and my mom." They pause. "And I haven't seen her in a while."

"Really?" Dee looks at Charlie. "Where is she?"

"Oh, she travels a lot for work," Charlie says. "She's a banshee, so she has to haunt the homes of people who are going to die soon. Or, as Mom calls them, the nearly departed."

"Wow," Dee says. Everyone knows haunting jobs are reserved only for the scariest monsters, which means Charlie's mom must be pretty terrifying. If Bella were here, Dee thinks, she would be impressed.

"Where does she have to travel?" Dee asks.

"All over the *world*." Charlie's voice is a funny mix of sadness and pride. "Sometimes she's away for months at a time." They lean in, lower their voice. "People don't always die when you think they're going to, you know."

As they round the corner to the checkout counter, Dee's foot collides with the open door of a dog crate, and she stumbles forward, sending the red ribbon, block of cheese, and fuzzy mice toys flying out of her arms. She reaches out to catch them but mistakenly fires off pink sparks instead.

The sparks hit the toys right before they reach the floor, and then the toys come alive. When the mice land on the floor, they scatter, leaving only the cheese—now a large, pungent block of aged Swiss—and the red ribbon in the center of the aisle.

Dee picks up the ribbon, the only toy that

didn't transform, and looks frantically around. Doing magic in a store run by humans is probably pretty high up on the Creepy Council's list of exilable offenses. "Did anybody see that?"

"No," Charlie says. "We're okay."

Suddenly three of the mice return, weaving through Dee's and Charlie's feet. They surround the cheese, then hoist it up onto their backs and scurry away together. Dee looks up.

A young girl, no more than two or three, has wandered away from her mom and into the aisle at the other end. She's staring at Dee.

Charlie frowns at Dee. "You're kind of clumsy with your magic, aren't you?"

She gives Charlie an awkward smile. She wishes she could be confident and sure of herself, the way Bella always is with her powers. But she isn't. "I'll just go and get some more toys."

Dee restocks on the cheese and fuzzy mice toys, and then she and Charlie get in line at the checkout counter. They're waiting behind a human woman holding a tiny poodle in her arms. When the poodle notices Charlie and Dee, it lets out a nervous little yip.

"So," Dee starts. "Where is your mom now?"

"Mexico," Charlie says. "That's where our family is from. She's living in some castle, haunting an old guy."

"She lives in a real castle?" Dee thinks about Bella again. No doubt she would find Charlie's mom to be just the creepiest. If she were here, she'd probably ask Charlie a bunch of questions. *What's the biggest scare your mom has ever pulled off? Does she prefer the shriek-and-freak method of scaring, or the silent-but-deadly? What's her favorite thing to wear when she scares, and how many blood-stains does it have?* And so on.

"That's why I have to live at YIKESSS, in the dorms," Charlie continues. "My mom's been away since the beginning of summer."

"Wait." At first Dee isn't sure she heard Charlie right. "You were living at the school by yourself for three months, while everyone else was home for summer break?"

Charlie nods.

Dee looks down at the cat toys, letting her dark curls fall over her face. She imagines what it would be like if she had to be away from Bella and her dads for three months.

"That must have been lonely," she says.

"It was," Charlie agrees, and then perks up a little. "But it wasn't all bad. Principal Koffin let me use the library, so I got to read basically whatever book I wanted."

Dee smiles sadly. Knowing Charlie has been by themself for an entire summer makes her feel terrible for complaining so much about Bella. So what if she and her sister fight sometimes? At the end of the day, Bella is her partner in crime and would do anything for her—even summon a storm cloud all the way from Seattle.

"Hey, Charlie," Dee says. "I want you to know you can always count on Bella and me." She shifts the pile of toys into her left arm and uses her right to reach for Charlie's hand. "You're not alone. Not anymore."

Charlie smiles, showing their fangs. "Thanks, Dee." They take Dee's hand in their own and squeeze it. "You guys are the creepiest friends I've ever had."

CHAPTER 8

The graveyard behind them is quiet as Bella and Eugene sit at the bus stop, waiting for the bus to arrive. The sun is nearing the horizon, making the shadows from the tombstones stretch longer and darker with every passing minute. If she listens closely, Bella can hear some grave ghosts in the distance, getting ready for another night of floating around.

Bella looks up at Eugene's pointy goblin ears. "You're not going to ride the bus like that, are you?"

"Hey," Eugene says, his ears drooping. "Goblins have feelings too."

"You know what I mean," Bella says. "You'll be recognized!"

They notice the bus in the distance, arcing over the hill. The headlights shine on the town sign, faded now with weather and age, that sits at the top of the hill:

WELCOME TO PECULIAR, PENNSYLVANIA!
A PERFECTLY NICE AND NOT-AT-ALL CREEPY PLACE TO LIVE

"Don't worry, Maleficent. This isn't my first rodeo." Eugene pulls a plain black beanie from the pocket of his blazer and puts it on his head, covering his ears and his poufy orange hair. He holds his hands out, like *ta-da*. "See? Now I'm human."

"Sure," Bella mutters to herself. "Because lots of humans have light green skin."

The bus slows to a stop in front of them, and the door squeaks open. Someone in a wide-brimmed hat and trench coat gets out. Bella and Eugene step past them, onto the bus. It's crowded, Bella notices irritably. All the seats are taken, so she and Eugene have to stand in the aisle and hang on to a pole to keep their balance.

When the bus starts moving, Bella looks out the window and notices that the person in the hat and trench coat has wandered into the graveyard. She watches them move clumsily around the tombstones and through the over-grown weeds. They stumble, and their hat falls off, revealing themselves to be not a person at all but a skeleton.

The bus careens around a corner, and Bella has to tighten her grip on the pole to keep from tumbling forward.

"Can I see the address again?" Eugene asks. Bella pulls a crumpled piece of paper from her pocket and hands it to him.

Eugene uncrumples it. "This is a note from Dad and Pop." He grins. "They call you 'Bella Boo'?"

Bella snatches the note out of his hands, then gives him the correct piece of paper.

"Okay," he says, studying it. "The market is five stops away, and then the mayor's house is two more from there." He looks at Bella. "I bet we can still get there before Cornelius."

"Shh," Bella says, glancing around. "Are you trying to tell the whole town about our secret?"

"Well, they wouldn't have known it *was* a secret until just now, when you called it one," Eugene points out.

The bus screeches to a stop, and a few people standing behind them squeeze past to get off.

"Holy hobgoblins," Eugene says. He lowers his voice. "Don't look now, but Gretchen Cauldronson is standing, like, *right* behind you."

Bella's eyes go wide. Besides the mayor, Gretchen Cauldronson is the last person she wants to see. Bella recalls the sound of Ms. Cauldronson's voice, shrill and threatening as she recited the yell-o-gram: *The Creepy Council demands that all members of the Maleficent family strive to be upstanding supernatural citizens who keep low profiles. If they fail to do so, or draw any more attention to our community in any way, we will have no choice but to enforce a permanent exile.*

If Ms. Cauldronson sees them now and figures out what they're up to, then that's it. Her family's lives will be ruined forever, and it will be all her fault.

"What do we do?" Eugene whispers. He pulls his beanie down as far as he can and faces forward.

"Did she see us?" Bella asks, racking her brain for a plan.

Eugene glances over his shoulder. "I don't think so."

"Let's keep it that way," Bella says. "Come on."

They start pushing through the crowd and walk to the front of the bus, away from Ms. Cauldronson, and then stumble when the driver slams on the brakes at the next stop. A few more people get off, and a group of four girls, laughing and carrying milkshakes, gets on. Bella notices the way they smirk at the YIKESSS uniforms as they pass by. When one of the girls accidentally makes eye contact, Bella does her best Bloody Mary impression.

The girl hurries away, and Eugene frowns at Bella. "Why did you do that?"

"They were judging us," Bella says. "I could feel it."

To the humans, YIKESSS is a highly elite private school that their children are not eligible to attend, no matter how many attempted donations or strongly worded letters they send. As a result, there's a bit of a town bias against those who do attend. (If only they really knew!)

Bella looks out the window and spots the pink neon sign for Scary Good Shakes. The line for milkshakes is out the door, which is no surprise. Bella thinks about Dee. Aside from cats, the strawberry milkshakes from Scary Good Shakes are her sister's favorite thing in the world.

"Uh-oh," Eugene says. He points behind Bella. "Look."

Bella turns to find that the girls and their milkshakes have found seats at the back of the bus. Now there's nobody shielding them from Gretchen Cauldronson's view.

"We're toast," Eugene whispers. "Burnt, crispy toast."

Bella looks around for anything that could help them, but all she sees are humans on their cell phones. She looks down at herself. "We need to take off our blazers. She's going to recognize them, if she hasn't already."

They quickly remove their blazers and hide them in their backpacks. Then Bella spots her pink eyephone at the bottom of the bag and lets out a tiny gasp.

"I know how to get Ms. Cauldronson off the bus," she says, pulling the phone out of the bag. "Follow my lead."

Bella dials *67 to hide her phone number, and then enters the number for the Creepy Council tip line. It rings once, twice, and on the third ring a voice answers.

"Creepy Council, Peculiar Chapter. What's your emergency?"

Bella thrusts the phone toward Eugene. His eyes widen.

"What am I supposed to say?" he whispers.

"I don't know," Bella whispers back. "Just think of something!"

"Uh, yes, hello there," he says, deepening his voice. "I'd like to report some strange . . . bigfoots outside my house."

Bella makes a face. *Bigfoots?* she mouths. Eugene just shrugs.

"I'm sorry, sir," the voice on the phone says. "Did you say 'bigfoots'?"

"Um, yes, I did," Eugene continues. "And they're all over the place, so if you could get somebody down here right away, I'd appreciate it."

"Certainly. What's the address of the residence?"

"Uh . . ." Eugene looks out the window. "Across the street from YIKESSS." Then he looks at Bella, who motions for him to hang up. "Oh no. One of them's got Grandma! Gotta go."

He hangs up and hands the eyephone back to Bella. "You think they bought it?"

"There's only one way to find out," Bella says. She peeks over her shoulder at Ms. Cauldronson, whose blueteeth have just started to chatter.

"YIKESSS is right up the road," Eugene says, ducking behind Bella. "If our plan works, she'll get off at the next stop."

Bella watches Ms. Cauldronson pull her blueteeth out of her purse and put them into her mouth. It doesn't take long for her perfect composure to morph into something more sinister. After a few more seconds stewing in silence, she reaches her arm up and yanks the cord on the wall, signaling for the driver to stop.

"It worked!" Bella says, suppressing a smile. "Okay, act natural. Like a human at the end of a long day."

Eugene slouches into the pole they're holding on to and closes his eyes, feigning exhaustion.

"No, not like that," Bella says. "That's too much. Be more . . . *nonchalant*."

Eugene stands up straighter and puts his hands into his pockets. He makes eye contact with a human across the aisle and gives them a little head nod.

"Eugene, no!" Bella snaps. "You're doing nonchalance wrong!"

"I'm trying my best," Eugene sighs, slouching again. "Humans have so many different emotions, it's hard to keep them all straight."

"Well, you need to try harder," Bella whispers.

"Okay, okay," Eugene mutters. He tries nonchalance again. "Jeez, you're pushy."

Bella opens her mouth to respond with something snarky, but nothing comes out. Earlier that day, in Principal Koffin's office, Dee said the exact same thing.

I would never even have conjured those flames in the first place if you hadn't distracted me. You're so pushy.

What had Bella said to distract her sister in Spell Casting? Something about Dee's form, how it looked like she was swatting a fly, but she can't remember exactly. She guesses that's the problem. She never thinks very much about the bad things she says until after they come out of her mouth.

Suddenly Bella feels terrible. She wishes she could be kinder and more careful with her words, the way Dee is when she talks to people. It's something Bella has always had trouble with.

The bus slows to a stop. Ms. Cauldronson

shuffles through the crowded bus toward the front exit. When she walks past Bella and Eugene, Bella holds her breath, bracing to be seen, but Ms. Cauldronson doesn't even flinch. She keeps her eyes straight ahead and walks off the bus.

"Hey, Maleficent," Eugene says, still practicing. "How's this?" He's leaning against the pole, looking bored and a little annoyed.

Bella smiles, grateful for the chance to try again.

CHAPTER 9

The sun has dipped below the horizon by the time the monsters make it to the mayor's house. Bella and Eugene, the first to arrive, scope out the property for the most advantageous place to hide. They settle behind a cluster of bushes on the left side of the house, under a window that looks into the mayor's dining room. A few minutes later Dee and Charlie appear, rounding the corner from Mulberry Drive, one street over.

The mayor lives in the biggest house in the middle of a perfectly plain human neighborhood. All the shrubs and fences look the same, the grass is no taller than the smallest fairy, and the houses are painted in the most boring shade of beige—a dreadful existence, it's safe to say.

Bella spots her sister and starts frantically waving her arms. "Over here!" she calls out, her voice somewhere between a whisper and a yell.

Dee and Charlie crouch down and run as quietly as they can to the bushes. When they meet up with the others, Dee holds out her arms and tackles Bella into a hug.

"I'm sorry!" they both say, laughing and squeezing each other tight.

"Thank badness," Eugene says. "It's about time you witches made up."

"Shh!" Charlie warns at the same time. They point at the big bay window that reveals the mayor's dining room. "Look."

They all peer over the bushes and look inside. The mayor and his family are sitting around the table, eating a dinner of what appears to be roast turkey, potatoes, and greens. The mayor is at one end of the table, his wife is at the other, and sitting between them, in the center by the turkey platter, is a boy.

Dee recognizes the boy instantly. She takes the Polaroid photo of Cornelius out of her pocket and holds it up to compare. He's a little older now, probably even the same age as Dee, but it's definitely him: the mayor's son.

"We know," Eugene says. "We've been keeping an eye on them in case Cornelius decides to make an appearance."

"He hasn't shown up yet?" Charlie says, a crease in their brow. "What if Bella was wrong, and he doesn't come?"

"I wasn't wrong," Bella assures them. Then

she sits up a little straighter and takes a deep breath. "What I mean to say is, just because Cornelius isn't here yet doesn't mean he won't come." She rests her hands on her knees and closes her eyes. "We are practicing *patience*, Charlie. It's the third *P*."

"Um . . ." Charlie gives her a strange look. "Okay. I just think—"

"There he is!" Dee points to the front yard. Sure enough, they all spot Cornelius's fluffy orange body slowly strutting up the stone pathway, heading toward the front door.

"Quick." Dee turns to Charlie. "Get the catnip!"

Charlie unzips their backpack and pulls out the shaker of catnip, plus a fuzzy mouse toy. Next to them Eugene pulls the tab on a can of tuna and cracks it open.

"Yuck," Dee says, plugging her nose.

"That's exactly the reaction we were hoping for," Eugene says. He looks at Charlie, a twinkle of excitement in his eye. "Okay, you stay here. I'll go around the other side of the house and meet you in front, in case Cornelius tries to go in that direction."

Without another word Eugene disappears into the darkness.

Charlie sighs. "Here goes nothing." They creep around the bush and start shaking the catnip. "Here, Cornelius!" they whisper. "Here, kitty, kitty!"

Bella and Dee exchange a wary look. For the first time since lunch, they have a moment alone.

"Dee, I really am sorry," Bella blurts out. "I shouldn't have criticized your technique in Spell Casting. If I'd just let you figure it out on your own, this day could have gone so much differently."

"You were just trying to help me," Dee says. She starts pulling at the grass around her feet. "And anyway, I'm glad it happened. If it hadn't, we might not have met Charlie and Eugene." She gives her sister a small smile.

"That's true," Bella says. "But it doesn't change the fact that you were right. I *was* being pushy."

"Maybe a little," Dee agrees. "But you were right too. I did need your help. My technique was off." The wind picks up, and Dee tucks her curls behind her ear. "You're way better at this witch stuff than I am."

Bella grins. The breeze lifts her long hair off her shoulders, and she lets it flow freely around her face.

"Only because I read the handbook." Bella takes Dee's hands between her own. "Don't you remember what Principal Koffin said? It's been *years* since she's met witches as powerful as us at our age. *Us.* You and me together."

They're interrupted, momentarily, by one of Charlie's sneezes.

"And besides," Bella says. "You're way better at making friends than me. We wouldn't be hanging out with Charlie and Eugene if it weren't for you."

Dee thinks, again, about stopping the earthquake in Principal Koffin's office, a spell so advanced that she could hardly believe it zapped from her own fingers. How did she do it? She remembers watching the heavy books fall around Bella, how each one only narrowly missed her sister's head, and she didn't think. She reached out a hand knowing only that she *needed* to save her sister. And then she did.

"I guess we do make a pretty good team," Dee says, squeezing her sister's hands.

"Come here, kitty!" they hear a frustrated Charlie say. "ACHOO!"

Bella peeks through the window just in time to notice the mayor perk up in his seat. Did he hear Charlie's sneeze? She leans around the bush, to where Charlie and Eugene are crouching in the shadows by the porch.

"Hurry up over there!" Bella says. "I think the mayor is getting suspicious!"

"We're trying!" Eugene whispers back. "But Cornelius isn't interested in the tuna."

"Or the catnip," Charlie adds. "See?" They shake the catnip again, and Cornelius doesn't even glance in their direction. He keeps scratching at the front door, waiting to be let inside.

"Try the red ribbon toy," Dee tells Charlie from her spot by the window. She peeks over the bush and into the dining room. "Okay, the mayor definitely hears something," she says to Bella. "He keeps turning his head toward the door."

"Make the cat stop scratching!" Bella hisses at Charlie and Eugene. "Just charge at him or something!"

"There's a security camera by the front door," Eugene says. "If we take one step onto the porch, we'll be seen."

"Jeepers creepers." Bella squeezes her eyes shut, struggling to come up with a plan. She listens to the wind whooshing through the air, hears the rhythmic scratching of Cornelius's paws against the hardwood, and is reminded of a ticking clock.

"Wait, Charlie!" She perks up. "You're a vampire. Do you even show up on camera?"

"Of course I do," Charlie scoffs. "Not everything you hear about vampires is true, you know."

"Right," Bella sighs. "Sorry."

"I don't ask if you have warts just because you're a witch, do I?" Charlie continues.

"Okay," Bella says. "Point taken."

Cornelius takes a break from scratching to let out a long, low meow. In the shadows Charlie and Eugene exchange a panicked glance.

"The mayor's son," Dee says, still keeping watch by the window. "He's pointing at the front door. He must have heard Cornelius meow." Her eyes go wide. "Oh! Now he's getting up."

"*And* the cat is scratching again," Eugene adds. "Creeptastic."

"Now is not the time for sarcasm, Eugene," Charlie says. "ACHOO!"

"He's walking to the door," Dee says, backing away from the window. "He's almost there."

Cornelius, sensing someone coming, stops scratching. He sits up straight and looks at the doorknob just as it begins to turn.

CHAPTER 10

Since the term "coven" persists through-
out literature and cinema as the preferred
way to describe reclusive groups of witches, it
may come as a surprise to learn that they don't
actually exist. With a few notable exceptions
(the Wicked Witch and the Blair Witch, for

example), most witches are, and have always been, fully functioning members of society.

The term "coven," as it pertains to witches, was popularized by a human, an English historian in the early twentieth century. Though most of what she wrote about witchcraft was wrong, one of her theories related to covens does hold true: witches are more powerful in pairs.

Indeed, it's common knowledge in the supernatural community that when two or more witches channel their magic together, usually through chanting or physical touch, their magic grows in strength. And the stronger the bond between the witches, the more powerful the magic.

Crouching in the bushes by the mayor's house, Bella's and Dee's green eyes brighten as they exchange a knowing look. They have only a few seconds to get Cornelius away from the front door before the mayor's son discovers him, which means there's only one thing left to do now.

Magic.

The twins grab hands and lock eyes. With their dark hair billowing around them in the breeze, they focus all their energy on Cornelius and removing him from the porch. They don't know if it will work—they've never tried channeling their magic before—but they know one thing for sure: no other two witches have a stronger bond than theirs.

Purple sparks appear at Bella's and Dee's fingertips and then snake down their hands, binding their wrists together. Suddenly a big, iridescent bubble appears around Cornelius and lifts him into the air. As the front door opens, the gusty wind quickly blows the bubble in their direction and then pops it, dropping the bemused cat right into Dee's arms.

The mayor's son sticks his head out of the doorway and looks around.

"Anyone there?" he calls out, and then lingers for a few moments, waiting. Everyone, including Cornelius, stays silent. After one final, careful glance at the bushes where Bella and Dee are hiding, the boy goes back inside and shuts the door.

The twins exhale the breath they were holding.

"We did it!" Bella shouts, and then clamps a hand over her mouth. "Sorry," she whispers, grinning behind her hand. "But, Dee, we did it!"

"Hmm?" Dee, hugging Cornelius in her arms, isn't paying attention to Bella. She nuzzles her cheek into the cat's fluffy orange body and smiles. "You are *so* cute."

"I hate to interrupt," Charlie says, returning to the shrubs, with Eugene at their side. "But let's get out of here before that boy comes back!"

Dee tightens her grip on Cornelius. The rest of the group collects the cat food, toys, and their belongings and the four friends scramble away, cutting across the next-door neighbor's yard and running down the block. They don't slow down until they turn the corner and arrive at the bus stop. Dee sits down on the bench with Cornelius, while Bella, Charlie, and Eugene huddle nearby, adrenaline still coursing through their veins.

"That was so wicked!" Eugene says. "I thought we were done for. How did you witches make that bubble?"

"We channeled our magic." Bella grins at Dee, who is still smiling down at Cornelius. "I knew we could do it."

"I'm glad *you* knew," Charlie says. "I, for one, was very close to having a full-on panic attack."

Eugene pats Charlie on the shoulder sympathetically. Then he says, "Hey, you're a fast runner, Charlie. Are you going out for track and field in the spring?"

Charlie shakes their head. "Too many afternoon races. I'd burn to a crisp."

"Good thing all the flyball games are at night," Bella adds.

Eugene and Charlie give her a curious look.

"What?" She shrugs. "I memorized the schedule."

A low, even rumbling sound starts coming from the bench where Dee sits.

"Aww," Dee coos. Cornelius is curled up in a ball and purring contentedly in her lap. "He likes me."

"Jeepers creepers." Bella turns back to Eugene and Charlie. "Well, we got the cat back. Assuming knocking it over the head is still out of the question—"

"It is," Dee says quickly.

Bella purses her lips. "So what do we do with him now?"

"Take him to the animal shelter?" Charlie suggests.

Bella shakes her head. "He's too recognizable. What if the mayor wants to adopt another cat, sees Cornelius, and gets suspicious?"

"I hate to say it," Eugene says, "but I think we should take him back to my parents. I'm guessing by now they've noticed he's missing, and probably also know that I had something to do with it."

Bella looks unsure. "Won't they be mad?"

"Oh, yeah," Eugene says. "Supremely. But at least if we bring him back, they can't be mad at me for losing the cat." He winces. "Only for breaking into the lab and letting my witch friend bring him back to life."

Bella smiles wide and claps her hands together. "You called me your friend!"

Eugene smirks. "Of course you're my friend, Maleficent," he says, throwing an arm around her shoulders. "It's like I said before. I like mischief of *all* kinds."

Down the block the bus turns the corner onto Mulberry Drive. Bella, Eugene, and Charlie search their pockets for their bus passes, while Dee scoops up Cornelius and puts him inside her backpack.

"Bella," Dee says, hoisting the bag onto her shoulders. "I was thinking. Maybe Eugene's parents and our dads would let *us* keep Cornelius?"

Bella snorts. "That cat is the reason we almost exposed all the monsters in Peculiar. No way are they going to let us keep it."

"Almost," Dee repeats. "We almost exposed them, but we didn't. We got Cornelius back, which means we actually *prevented* a sure disaster, don't you think?"

"Yeah!" Eugene shouts. "That's good. Keep saying stuff like that when we get back to my place."

They board the bus and find a cluster of seats in the back. While Dee whispers reassurances to Cornelius through her backpack, and Eugene and Charlie debate the pros and cons of the bubble as a method of transportation, Bella thinks about the human girls from earlier that day. She remembers the way they all laughed together, how it seemed like they were having so much fun, and how jealous it made her feel. Now Bella looks around the bus at Dee, Eugene, and Charlie and realizes she doesn't feel jealous anymore. She has everything she needs right in front of her.

Well, almost.

"Hey," Bella says, and they all look at her. "I've got an idea."

Twenty minutes later they're standing out-side Scary Good Shakes, milkshakes in hand.

"I don't know about you ghouls," Eugene says, slurping his triple-chocolate milkshake with fudge drizzle. "But that was the wildest first day of school I've ever had."

"Are you kidding?" Bella plucks the cherry off the top of her milkshake and pops it into her mouth. "This was the wildest day of my *life*."

"Welcome to YIKESSS," Charlie says, stirring their vanilla shake with extra whipped cream. "Where wild stuff happening is just another Monday."

"I really hope not," Dee says between sips of her strawberry shake. She went through more in one day at YIKESSS than she'd been through in five years at the human school. She was very much looking forward to a calmer year ahead. "But hey." She links arms with Charlie. "What-ever happens, we'll get through it together."

"Cheers to us!" Bella holds up her shake, and the rest of the group follow along.

"And to our awesome friendship," Dee adds. In her backpack Cornelius lets out a low meow.

"And a fun but *hopefully* less eventful school year," Charlie says. Bella and Dee nod in agreement.

Eugene yanks his shake back. "I will not say 'cheers' to a less eventful school year! I'm just getting started!" He pauses and takes a quick sip. "In fact, I was thinking about another invention while we were standing in line. Picture this: a skateboard ramp that also cooks grilled cheeses." He looks around eagerly at his friends. "I'll call it the CheezySkate 6000."

Charlie raises an eyebrow. "Why do all your inventions end in '6000'?"

Eugene shrugs. "It's my favorite number."

Bella laughs. "Fine." She holds up her shake again. "Cheers to us, our friendship, and the CheezySkate 6000."

The monsters lift their milkshakes triumphantly into the air.

CHAPTER 11

A few days have passed since the escape of Cornelius the undead cat and the narrowly avoided public relations disaster with the mayor. Fortunately, no more floods, earthquakes, or accidental revivals have occurred at the young witches' hands since. Save for the cherry Jell-O incident (Bella tried to zap her broccoli into dessert and accidentally hit the kitchen table instead—the results were messy), the rest of the week has been rather calm.

Now it's a sunny Thursday afternoon in the Maleficent twins' bedroom. Bella is in the closet, trying on her brand-new scream team uniform, and Dee is finishing some homework on her bed, having enchanted her pencil so it does the writing for her. Cornelius, looking dapper in his new green collar, is cuddled up in Dee's lap. When he starts to purr, Dee looks away from her pencil, letting it fall, so she can kiss him on the top of his head.

"I'm going to love you forever," she whispers. That's how long he's going to live now that he's undead.

Cornelius meows contentedly and then adjusts his position, so his belly is in the air for Dee to scratch.

While Eugene's mother and father were certainly upset that he and his friends broke into the lab and zapped Cornelius back to life, they agreed the best thing for everyone was to let Dee keep him—on one condition. Bella and Dee had to channel their magic to change the cat's fur from a fluffy orange into a sleek black to prevent him from being recognized by the mayor in the future. To this the twins happily agreed.

As for the issue of Mayor Boris Smith himself, Eugene's parents took care of that, too, claiming a rather gruesome taxidermy incident that prevented them from preserving poor Cornelius. They gave the mayor a refund, as well as a hefty discount on his next deceased pet.

Dee is finishing a worksheet for her Potions Brewing class when she looks up and notices a spider on her headboard. Small, black, and spindly, it's crawling down the left bedpost, toward her pillow. She screams and jumps off the bed, sending a startled Cornelius flying through the air. He lands on Bella's bed on all fours, then lets out an irritated little *mew*.

Bella comes running out of the closet they

share. She's wearing her green-and-black scream team uniform, plus one sneaker. "What is it?"

Dee hides behind Bella and points to her headboard. "There's a spider!"

"Oh, jeepers creepers," Bella snaps. "It's just a little bug."

Dee shakes her head quickly. "It's got *way* too many legs."

Bella sighs. She holds out a hand toward the spider and thinks about encasing it in a bubble, the same way she did Cornelius. Purple sparks shoot from her fingertips, and the bubble appears around the spider.

"Creepy," Dee says, eyes wide.

Bella grins. "I've been practicing." With her arm extended she floats the bubble through the air and out the open second-story window. She lets it drift down into the herb garden and then pop, gently dropping the spider onto a leaf.

The twins stick their heads out the window.

They see one of their dads, Antony, picking some rosemary (for dinner) and demon root (for werewolf bunions). In the yard behind him, by a giant wooden skateboard ramp, are Eugene and Charlie.

Eugene's parents didn't ground him, and they didn't ask Bella and Dee's dads to give them any money for Cornelius, either. All they wanted in return was to make sure any future hijinks occurred at Bella and Dee's house. Eugene's parents were, after all, still repairing the ceiling from last month's indoor waterslide fiasco.

Bella and Dee watch as Eugene sits in the center of the ramp and hammers together two pieces of wood, while Charlie stands off to the side, wringing their hands.

"Are you sure this is structurally sound?" Charlie says, inspecting one part of the ramp Bella and Dee can't see. "There's a big gap here."

"Yeah, I know. That's where the grilled

cheese machine is going to go." Eugene stops hammering and looks at Charlie. "Hey, might wanna reapply some Sunscream. Your nose is looking almost as red as your eyes."

Charlie touches the bridge of their nose and winces. "Thanks."

"Hey, Dad," Bella calls out from the window. Antony looks up. "Can Charlie and Eugene stay for dinner?"

"Of course, Bella Boo," he says. Antony is an excellent cook, which is a rare feat for ghosts, since they don't actually need to eat. "As soon as Pop gets back from work, we're having rosemary chicken and pasta."

"Mmm," Dee says. Next to her, Cornelius hops up onto the windowsill and meows in agreement.

"No garlic for me, please, Mr. M!" Charlie yells as they slather their face in Sunscream. "I'm really allergic."

"I remember, Charlie," Antony replies. "No nuts either, right?"

"Right," Charlie says. Then they look at the ground and smile.

"Hey, witches," Eugene calls out. "What are you waiting for? Come check this out!"

Bella skips to the closet and slips on her left sneaker. Then she raises an eyebrow at Dee. "Well?"

Dee glances at her homework, still unfinished on her bed, and considers.

"Eh." She shrugs. "I can finish that later."

"Last one there has to clean Cornelius's litter for a week!" Bella says.

"He doesn't *poop*," Dee replies. "He's undead!"

But both sisters take off anyway. Laughing, they race down the stairs and out the door to the backyard, with Cornelius right on their heels. They don't stop running until they reach the ramp.

"I won!" Bella says when they make it to the ramp.

"Did not," Dee says. "You got a head start."

"Did not!" Bella stomps her foot, conjuring

red sparks with her heel. Suddenly the pieces of wood Eugene hammered together turn to liquid in his lap.

"Aw, no," Eugene groans. "Now it looks like I peed."

Bella and Dee exchange a glance, covering their mouths to hide their giggles. Then Dee, who's been doing some practicing of her own, conjures orange sparks, sending a steady breeze in Eugene's direction to dry his pants.

The young witches may not have a handle on their magic yet, and they may not have adoring-crowd levels of popularity, but they have good friends. And each other.

READ ON FOR A SNEAK PEEK AT
THE TWINS' NEXT THRILLING (MIS)ADVENTURE!

A widely believed myth among humans is that only witches and wizards practice alchemy, when in fact any supernatural creature with a proclivity for chemistry or botany can become a master of the craft. Take, for instance, Antony Maleficent. As a human, he was a respected pharmacologist who worked in a lab with medicines and chemicals. He also loved to cook, and as such, maintained a thriving herb and vegetable garden in his backyard. After the unfortunate lab explosion that turned him into a ghost, Ant took his skills with plants and chemicals and applied them to alchemy.

Ant traveled all around the world to learn everything he could, and then he settled in Peculiar, Pennsylvania, to start a family and open up his own apothecary—or pharmacy, according to the humans. He mixes, measures, and concocts all the potions and prescriptions himself while his partner, Ron, takes care of the finances. His twin daughters, the young witches Bella and Donna Maleficent, sometimes help out by unpacking inventory or stocking shelves.

It's a brisk fall afternoon on a Monday in Peculiar when one of the twins is doing just that.

Gray clouds hang low over the little black storefront at the end of Main Street, just past the Manor movie theater and across from Bethesda's Broom Shoppe. A neon sign that reads ANT & RON'S hangs proudly over the door, enchanted with a blue light that will never burn out. Inside, the front room resembles a regular pharmacy, complete with aisles of human products, a cash register, and a counter where customers pick up their prescriptions. There's a small waiting area in the corner, where Bella currently sits on a lounge chair, listening to music and scrolling through her eyephone. She still hasn't changed out of her scream team uniform from practice after school.

In the back room, where monsters shop, Donna is unpacking new shipments of both the human and supernatural variety. She's wearing her own black lab coat, a mini version of her dad Ant's work uniform. So far she has catalogued antibiotic ointment, eye of newt, sunscreen, *and* Sunscream, and she still has four more boxes to go.

Dee tucks her curls behind her ear and looks up at her cat, Cornelius. He's stretched out on his back on a top shelf, batting a green dust bunny back and forth between his paws. "Can I get a little help here?" she asks him. "You could use your claws to cut the rest of the boxes open."

Cornelius looks at her upside down, blinks once, and then returns his full attention to the dust bunny.

Dee sighs. The whole reason she has extra shifts at the pharmacy this week is because Cornelius scratched up one of the paintings in the foyer, the one with the weird-looking elephants. It had been given to Ant as a gift by an old friend named Salvador, and apparently was sort of priceless.

Dee rips open a new box and removes the packing tissue to find it stuffed with snakeskins. She jumps back and wrinkles her nose. "Why couldn't it have been cough drops?" she mutters.

Dee hears a bell chime in the distance, meaning a customer has come into the store. She moves to the door that connects the front and back rooms and looks through the small window there. She sees Bella on her phone, scrolling with her thumb and swaying her head to whatever music is coming through her earbuds, but Dee doesn't see anybody else.

"Dad," she calls out. "The bell rang. I think we have a customer."

When Ant doesn't reply, Dee leans back and peers through the doorway into his office. He has the phone perched between his chin and shoulder, and he's scribbling something down on a notepad. From this distance the makeup he applied to make his translucent skin appear less see-through almost makes him look human.

Dee turns to Cornelius. "I'm going to see if there's a customer who needs help. Be right back, okay?" She pauses by the door. "And *don't* break anything. If you do, I'm taking away your red ribbon for a week."

Cornelius gives her a startled look as she pushes open the door.

At first the store seems empty. Dee considers that maybe there's a ghost somewhere. They tend to make themselves completely invisible around humans to avoid any scrutiny. She stands still at the end of aisle two, listening, but hearing nothing except faint jazz music coming through the speakers on the ceiling. It's the "Smooth Jazz" playlist, Ant's favorite. If her pop, Ron, were managing the store today, they'd be listening to the Grateful Dead or Fleetwood Mac instead.

Dee is about to return to the back when she hears something coming from aisle four. She peeks around the corner and discovers a tall, gangly boy with dark brown skin flipping through a magazine. His curly hair pokes out from beneath his baseball cap, which features a logo of the Peculiar Porcupines, the mascot of the town's human public school.

Her eyes go wide as she realizes two things at once: the boy is the mayor's son, who almost caught her with Cornelius the night Bella zapped the cat back to life, and the magazine he's flipping through is *Haunted Housekeeping*, which was definitely not supposed to be in the front room, where humans could see it. She must have shelved it there by mistake.

Dee freezes behind the sunglasses display, unsure what to do next. Bella keeps insisting that nobody saw them that night, but what if Bella is wrong? What if the boy came here to tell them he knows exactly who they are and what they did?

She watches his expression as he flips through the magazine. He doesn't *look* scared or angry, or confused about the contents of the magazine. Actually, he looks interested. Then he laughs at something, and the sight of his smile makes every single bat in Dee's stomach take flight.

"What are you doing?"

Dee jumps and turns to find Bella standing behind her with only one earbud in her ear. Faintly Dee can hear the chorus of the Michael Jackson song "Thriller."

"Shh!" Dee switches places with Bella and then motions for her to look around the corner. "It's the mayor's son."

When she sees him, Bella's eyes narrow suspiciously. "What is *he* doing here?" She grabs a heart-shaped pair of sunglasses from the display case and puts them on. A crease of concern forms between her eyebrows. "Do you think it has something to do with Cornelius? What if he recognizes us?"

Dee bites her lip. She's thinking about the camera on the mayor's porch. Could there have been others in the bushes that they didn't see? She picks up a pair of rainbow sunglasses and puts them on like Bella.

"Well," Bella says. "There's only one way to know for sure." She looks back at Dee. "We'll have to wipe his memory from that night."

Dee nearly exposes their position by laughing out loud, but Bella claps a hand over Dee's mouth just in time. "You can't be serious," Dee mumbles from behind Bella's hand. She pushes the hand away and lowers her voice to a whisper. "You know doing magic on a human without the approval of the Creepy Council is, like, *way* forbidden. And even if it weren't, that's an advanced spell. It's not like we can just flip open the handbook to find it."

"I'm sure we could find it in one of Dad's and Pop's old books," Bella says. Her voice is calm, but even through sunglasses, Dee can see how Bella's eyes spark with trouble. "Eugene could help us pick the lock on the cabinet."

Ant and Ron's second-floor study contains a number of odds and ends that are strictly off-limits to the twins, but nothing is more untouchable than the dark purple cabinet behind Ant's desk. Protected with three different magic-proof dead bolts, this cabinet is known to the twins as the Cabinet of Doom, because their dads have always told them that if they ever dare to break the locks and venture inside, doom is what awaits them. Bella suspects the threat is just a scare tactic to keep them away from some really powerful spell books Ant collected while traveling the world to study alchemy, but Dee is slightly less certain.

What if the cabinet contains an orb that conjures her worst fears, or a black hole that zaps her somewhere terrible? Either way, spiders would surely be involved.

Dee crosses her arms and sneaks another peek at the human. "He could get hurt."

"He won't," Bella says. "At least, not if we do the spell correctly."

"Have a heart, Bella," Dee says, shaking her head. "He just lost his cat! Don't you think he's been through enough?"

"Why do you care?" Bella takes off her sunglasses. She knows Dee has always been a softie when it comes to humans, but Dee has never taken such a keen interest in the well-being of one before. "He's just some random human."

"Excuse me?"

The twins turn their heads in unison. Standing in front of them is the mayor's son, holding the issue of *Haunted Housekeeping* and looking right at Dee.